The
Can

Consultants

Ashley Bishop, Ed.D.

Sue Bishop, M.E.D.

Publishing Credits

Dona Herweck Rice, *Editor-in-Chief*

Robin Erickson, *Production Director*

Lee Aucoin, *Creative Director*

Tim J. Bradley, *Illustrator Manager*

Janelle Bell-Matin, *Illustrator*

Sharon Coan, *Project Manager*

Jamey Acosta, *Editor*

Rachelle Cracchiolo, M.A.Ed., *Publisher*

Teacher Created Materials

5301 Oceanus Drive

Huntington Beach, CA 92649-1030

http://www.tcmpub.com

ISBN 978-1-4333-2926-5

van

I see a van.

man

I see a man.

can

I see a can.

pan

I see a pan.

The man has a can and a pan.

Glossary

can

man

pan

van

Sight Words

I   see   a
The   has   and

Extension Activities

Read the story together with your child. Use the discussion questions before, during, and after your reading to deepen your child's understanding of the story and the rime (word family) that is introduced.

The activities provide fun ideas for continuing the conversation about the story and the vocabulary that is introduced. They will help your child make personal connections to the story and use the vocabulary to describe prior experiences.

Discussion Questions
- Where is the van in the story? What other cars have you seen besides a van?
- What do you think is in the can that the man buys at the store? Do you like food that comes in a can? Why or why not?
- What do we use a pan for at home?
- What else can the man cook in his pan?

Activities at Home
- Go into the kitchen with your child. Talk about the different cans and pans that are found in the kitchen. As you find these items, review the -*an* rime in both words.
- Who is a man in your family? Talk with your child about the different men in both your immediate and extended family. Make a list of these men with the title, *I See a Man.*